SONG
OF A RED
MORNING

A SHORT STORY
OF DARK-AGE
SCOTLAND

BARBARA LENNOX

COPYRIGHT

DEDICATION

To my late parents, who gave me that greatest of gifts, a love of reading.

TABLE OF CONTENTS

Map of Southern Scotland in the Late Iron Age

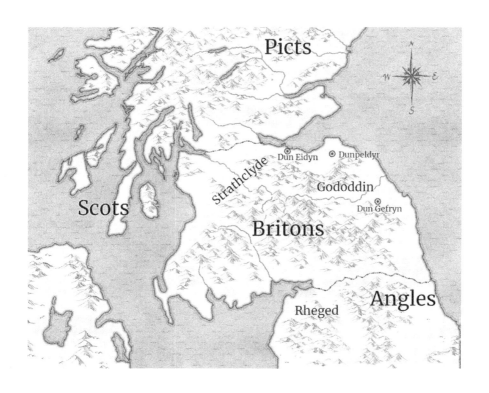

Picts

Scots

Strathclyde

Dun Eidyn ⊚ ⊚ Dunpeldyr

Gododdin

Dun Gefryn ⊚

Britons

Rheged

Angles

SONG OF A RED MORNING

*W*e should never have come here!

The thought catches me unawares, and I wonder if some demon of despair, spawned by the summer of defeat, has lodged itself within my heart. But no, it is only the fog and the night and the cold that saps my spirit and my pride.

Beside me, on Dunpeldyr's rampart, my father, Amlawdd, peers into the fog and leans forward, listening.

'Do you hear it, Gweryn?'

I cease my pacing and listen too, but I hear nothing; no sound of men approaching, no muted knock of metal, no muffled oath in a foreign tongue. All sounds are stolen into ghosts and I hear only the whisper of wind in the grasses and the anxious thudding of my heart.

'There is nothing to hear,' I say. 'They will not come before the dawn and that is many hours hence. But what a dawn it will be! As red as the ears of Arawn's hounds. As red as the blood of the Angles!'

My brave words fall like stones into a well, but he nods in agreement. Both of us know how red the dawn will be. Red with our own blood flowing in the sunlight.

We should never have come here! my heart cries, but my head tells me otherwise, for we had no choice. The Angles besiege Dun Eidyn now, and they say high Dun Gefryn is burned and ruined, so we cannot look for help from there. Here we have come and here we must make our stand, for no other way is open to us, none but the one of which we do not speak, and the silence falls between us like a sword.

I look around the fort, at the great ramparts of Dunpeldyr on which my men stand guard. Only the smoking torches fading into distance show its extent – the mighty fortress of the Votadini in the land of Gododdin, a place of strength and might and song. Yet it is empty now and only we remain, the remnants of the war-host that rode from these walls so proudly so many defeats ago. The women and children have gone to the summer pastures in the hills, the shielings among the heather, and this year they have taken everything, the ox-carts and the flocks, the cattle and the breeding mares, the priests and their gilded crosses – all our treasures. So now the fort echoes, even in the fog, dark save for torches on the walls and the fires by the huts where men who can sleep find oblivion in dreams.

We should never have come here! But my men were tired and hungry, some of them hurt and all of them afraid. It seemed a refuge, a rock to cling to in the rising tide of enemies from the East who have crept up the river with the fog. But now, in the bitter cold of a thick autumn night, with the Angles camped below the walls, it seems to me it is a trap that will become a tomb.

'We will hold Dunpeldyr,' I say, forcing myself to remember that tides ebb as well as flow. 'We have men enough, supplies for a month at least. And in a month the Angles will have gone.'

My father looks at me. Does he believe the words I speak to the men? All my skills have deserted me, my stratagems, my battle-cunning, but still this remains: the ability to make men believe in a leader who has long since ceased to believe in himself. And I must lead them when the dawn comes, fifty men from the hundred who rode singing into the spring, fifty to fight in a morning red with blood.

Amlawdd shakes his head. 'Not this year, my son. This year the Angles have come to stay, and they will not leave these walls until the last of us is dead and ravens tear at our flesh.'

I know. *I know!* But I do not want to hear it. 'Then what would you have us do?' I ask, angry now. 'Yield Dunpeldyr? If we yield this place then we cannot defend our lands.'

And this, of course, is the heart of the matter. The one treasure we cannot send to the hills with the ox-carts and our families. The land itself. Even in the darkness I am aware of the expanse of it, this land of Gododdin that gave me birth, the farmland and the forests, the copses by the river, the meadows and the foothills of the moors, the land we have named, the place that has shaped us. It is as much part of me as are my bones, and I feel its desecration as if it is my own skin that crawls with Angle filth. I shudder with the fear that we have already lost the lands to the foreign horde. I shudder and pretend it is with the cold. I draw my cloak around me for warmth, but it is heavy with moisture. Beneath the wool, the metal links of my mail are icy through my linen tunic, and the silver bands around my wrists chill me still further. My gold torque seems to choke me now, and my sword hangs heavy at my side. Only the silver cross I wear on a thong of leather is warm against my skin, but it brings little comfort.

Amlawdd leans forwards to listen once more, and this time I hear it too, a distant chanting, a drumbeat that trembles more in the earth than in the air, a wailing droning melody and the sound of voices singing in their tuneless foreign tongue. The Angles are singing!

'What have they to sing about!' A sick anger wells up in my throat. I spit my anger into the wind and my hand tightens on the leather grip of my spear until my nails draw blood from my palm. But then, from further along the wall, one of my men lifts his voice in defiance and others join him as they sing of the massacre of Maescelynn, a song from my grandfather's day of how the war-band of Dunpeldyr rode a raiding party of Angles into the river and killed them all. *And thrice more did the thirsty spears of Connawl drink deep their fill, Connawl, hard-handed, hewer of men. For thrice three nights did ravens feast . . .*

My spirits lift with the voices. I was reared on such tales of pride and prowess. They are as much a part of me as the blood in my veins, as the land in my bones. They are our histories, our reason to be here. They are the power behind our sword arms, the steel to strengthen our uncertain hearts. While the song lasts the grim spectre of defeat vanishes into the fog, and I know the Votadini can never be defeated. We will prevail in the morning, or we will die. But such a death will be its own song.

I grin at my father, but he just shakes his head. 'The Angles sing of the same things as we do. They sing the stories of their peoples. They sing of victories and – '

'Victories?' Still the song holds me and his words stir a reckless anger. 'We will give them nothing of victory to boast of in their middens! Not now, not ever!'

He reaches out to grip my arm then jerks me around to face him.

'They already have their victory. They have taken the lands. They have not come to raid as once they used to. They come to settle now. They leave the peasants to till the soil and fish the seas. Our people give their tribute to the Angles now, not to us. We have nothing left to defend, Gweryn, nothing but a fort they do not want. We should go while there is still time, go West and –'

'No!' I wrench my arm from his grip, afraid that he might persuade me of the course he has refused to speak of until now, for it is the way of cowards. 'Go West, you say, pledge ourselves to the Selgovae and fight their battles. In exchange for what? A few wind-swept heather-choked valleys and the chance to starve? On land we cannot even call our own? No! This is the land of the Votadini. Gododdin is our land, Dunpeldyr our stronghold.'

'And whose land was it before we took it? Who were the peoples who farmed it before we came? Who hunted in our hunting runs? What was their name? We do not know, Gweryn, because, like you would have us do, they tried to hold it for their own – and failed. No-one sings of failure.'

So we must not fail. We will hold, or die such a death that even the Angles will tell of it in their strongholds. I am not afraid of death. No, I fear other things. I turn away, climb down from the rampart and walk to the great iron-bound gate of seasoned oak. I reach out and touch it, feel the texture of wood hewn from our forests. How old is this gate? How many men have ridden through its portals, singing in the morning as we did? As we will do, come the dawn. It holds our history, this wood, this gate. It is solid beneath my hand and almost warm, a comfort when there are few comforts to be had. My father comes to join me by the gate and puts a hand on my shoulder, but I shake him off.

'This is our land,' I say, my voice as hard and unyielding as the gate. 'We fought for it once and we have held it since. Even when the Romans came we held it for our own. They built no forts in our land, nor roads, for they did not dare. Who of all the peoples of the Lands between the Walls can claim as much? And you say we should give up what we have held in pride for so long? No. To me was given the ordering of this battle. Not you, old man. And I say we stand. If you have not the stomach for the fight then you should have gone with the wagons, sneaked into the night with other old men, the priests and children and women.'

'Not all the women!'

I turn and see Ermid standing close by, smiling at me.

'I thought you asleep,' I say.

'How can I sleep when my husband will not? How can I sleep when dogs howl beyond the walls?' Her voice is amused. 'Do you hear them, Gweryn? The Angles – singing!'

'My father would have it that they sing of victory!' I make my voice as light and amused as hers. I will not have her know I share my father's fears. She laughs and it twists my heart. *I should not have brought her here!* And then I smile at the foolishness of my thought. As if I can command her! I would have had her go with the ox-carts and the other women, but she had laughed at that too.

'Am I not a shield-maiden of the Votadini? Can I not fight for my people and my land and my chieftain? I will fight by your side, my husband, and if you fall then I will stand over your body until they hack me to the ground. They will know thereby that you are a chief of men!'

A fierce woman, my wife. Fierce and proud. She terrifies me. She is the smoke in my blood, the wellspring of my fear. She is my soul.

'My father would have it that we should slip away and go into the West,' I say, voicing the possibility for her consideration.

'And where would be the song in that?' she asks, turning to Amlawdd in surprise.

'At least there would be a song to sing and people to sing it!' He is angry now, for he knows I will hold by Ermid's decision.

'We do not sing defeat,' I insist.

He turns his face from me and, in a flare of torchlight, I see how old he has become, a man beyond his prime. But, like Ermid, he would not go with the wagons when I urged him. I am a man plagued by the disobedience of those who love me. I throw my head back as if to look at the sky, but in truth it is because bitter moisture stings my eyes. Yet in that moment there is a turning of the air and the fog tears apart on a tongue of wind. Far above, netted in cloud, I see the stars, high and clear and careless of the realms of men. Then they are gone as the fog swirls back, thicker now, smearing the smoking torches into a gauzy web of leaden air. For a moment, the fort vanishes. Above us on the rampart the singing of the men falters until there is only one sound left, Rhuawn, our bard, plucking a harp. But the strings of woven horse-hair have gone slack with moisture and the notes fall to the ground like the mournful music of the other worlds of which the priests forbid us to speak. The gate, the strong iron-bound gate of seasoned oak, seems insubstantial now and looms through the fog like a threshold onto a world of ghosts and fell creatures of the night. I shiver, no longer with the cold, and the hairs on my arm rise. I am afraid, suddenly, of death. Of failing. Of diminishing. Of being forgotten.

'Come,' my father says, his hand on my arm, warm and comforting. I feel the urge to weep on his shoulder. 'Come. There is something you should see before the morning. Both of you. Come.'

We go with him, Ermid and I, to one of the lesser huts that was once used for storage. It is empty now, for everything that could be carried has been taken. But my father sweeps the straw from the floor and prises away the beaten earth with his dagger to reveal two planks of wood, the lid of an ancient chest. He takes his spear, wedges it in the crack between the planks and, grunting with the effort, heaves them apart.

There, bright in the torchlight, is a hoard of silver, tarnished and damaged but still beautiful. There are fragments of a gold-chased dish, a dented flagon, pieces of arm-rings pale as moonlight, and bent crosses set with carnelians and pearls. It is a mighty hoard, and yet I did not know of its existence!

'How came this here?' I ask. 'In what great battle was this won? Who did we defeat?'

'It was we who were defeated, Gweryn,' he says. 'It was a bribe given to us by the Romans.'

Ermid had crouched down and reached out a hand to touch the silver, but at Amlawdd's words she snatches it back and looks up at him. 'A bribe? The Votadini do not take bribes!'

'We did once, Ermid,' he tells her. 'In exchange for the peace to farm our lands, for blindness when their armies came. We looked aside when they fired the forts of our kinsmen, and we held the peace they bought from us when they marched South again. They promised us silver, a weight of silver so great it was impossible to imagine. Perhaps we thought they would play us false, and thus free us from our bargain, but they gave us what you see here – broken bowls and bent shards of things that had once been beautiful. The weight was as they promised. They kept their side of the bargain and laughed as they did so.'

Why do I not know of this? Why is this tale not told? But then I understand. It is the secret shame of the line of chieftains, a treachery that runs in my veins too, a shadow on our rule. My father has held it in his heart until tonight when he gives it to me to share. I understand why that is too.

'We should have flung it into the sea and killed them all!' says Ermid, fiercely.

'Yes. Perhaps there would have been a song in that. But we did not. We took their silver, and we have kept it, untouched, to remind us of what we did. Not all our history is locked within the poems of the bards. There are other memories of which we do not sing, for they are not a matter of pride. So are our lands held by right? Lands bought with broken silver? I think not. We have no right to hold these lands. We have no need to try.'

The strength goes from my bones. The land, my pride, my soul's rejoicing, slips from me on a torrent of tarnished silver. I sink to my knees before the hoard and drop my face into my hands, and my father touches me lightly on the shoulder.

'We are a people, Gweryn, a Tribe. We do not own the land or deserve it any more than those who came before us. We need not stay here and spill our blood for nothing more than pride in songs that do not tell the truth. We can go, take the silver with us, buy men and horses if that is what you want, come back in the spring and drive the Angles into the sea, or try to. But let us not waste our lives in the morning for false pride.'

But I no longer have any pride, false or otherwise, and now it is too late. I rise to my feet, thrust him back and make an angry useless gesture of denial.

'Cover it up again. Let it lie, here in Dunpeldyr where the Votadini rule. Let the Angles try to take it if they will.' I turn and stride out into the darkness again. Ermid runs after me, but she says nothing, and there are angry tears on her face.

My father is right. They will not find the silver for they do not want our fort. They will set fire at the gates and the stockades will burn, the huts, the stables, the church, the great hall. It will be a morning red with fire, but a day of ash blowing on the wind, and we will not see the sunset. We should have gone West, run to the kin we once betrayed, made our way by the high moors to Strathclyde, or to Rheged to join Urien and his sons. Anywhere. Anything but stay here for the sake of the last verse in a song no-one will ever hear.

I look up at the sky once more. The mist has cleared here on the heights, although the fog still lies thick below the walls. I can see the stars once more and I search them out and judge the coming of the dawn and the battle my pride has forced us to. There is an hour still. There is time.

'Are they still singing?' I shout up to the ramparts.

'Yes, lord,' a voice replies.

'Then let the Votadini sing! Sing the battle-songs of Gododdin! Let our voices rise above the mists and fogs to quail the hearts of the Angles! Let us make them fear the morning!'

I raise my spear above my head and shake it in defiance. Above me on the ramparts the men beat their shields with their swords or crash their spear-butts into the wall. Their voices rise, thundering into the night, and below us, hidden in the fog, a growl rises to a roar like a winter storm booming on shingle. Drums beat and the Angles chant. To the East, faint as starlight, dawn begins to silver the sky.

My father comes to stand beside me. He has tried and failed and now he regrets showing me the silver, as he regrets being shown himself. He too lost his pride, as I have lost mine. But he says nothing and I reach out and pull him close to me. 'Do you hear them father? Do you hear how many there are? How much noise they make!' I try to laugh, but it is a joyless sound. My heart has swelled and burst with the weight of fear and despair. 'So they will not hear us when we go,' I say softly, then raise my voice again, calling to the men. Quickly!' I shout. 'Before dawn comes! To the horses! To the western gate! We must ride into the West! So sing, you men of Dunpeldyr! Sing!' My voice breaks.

'We'll come back,' Ermid says, and her arms enfold me, my fierce wife, still proud, no longer of a land and a history but, miraculously, still of me. 'We'll fight here again!' I nod, but both of us know we will not.

My men fall silent and, one by one, the bridles of their horses muffled with strips of cloth, they leave the fort, slipping into the fog and leaving their comrades singing until only Ermid and I remain, our voices ragged and uncertain on the wind. I unbar the gate and stand there for a moment, thinking that I will stay and make a song of my ending. But Ermid takes my hand, and together, leading our horses, we too slip through the hidden western gate. Below us, beyond the walls, the Angles hear our song falter and fade to nothing. They think we are afraid and they jeer and beat their drums, chanting their heathen songs in their foreign tongue as they prepare themselves to attack.

But we have gone, riding down the narrow track between the moon-pale birches, slipping unseen between the outposts of the Angles, the faint sounds of our passing drowned by their chanting, as we slip West like the ghosts we have become.

I know what they will find in the morning – an empty fort wreathed in mist, the great gates lying open, a place of shadows and dreams and memories, with a bitter wind humming on the ramparts like the notes of a badly tuned harp. All we have left is a torch or two, guttering to smoke. The Angles will pause, swords and axes shifting in hands that are suddenly slick with a cold sweat. The hairs will rise on their necks for they too know of the other worlds, of hosts that vanish into the mists with their pale kings and spectral horses, and they will be afraid.

Behind us, in my mind's eye, one grasps a torch and flings it to the ground where it flares to flame. Another throws a burning branch into a hut where the straw catches alight. The muttering grows to a roar as they set fire to the fort, and the roar of men is drowned by the roar of flame as the huts and the stables burn. As the gate and the great hall of feasting burn down to ash.

They will not find the silver.

We are leagues away, the remnant of the Votadini, riding into the West to join our kin, leaving our lands behind, our histories fading. But we are singing as we go. Behind us the sun rises in the East and burns away the mists. Behind us the dawn is red with fire.

HISTORICAL NOTE

Gweryn, Amlawdd and Ermid are fictional characters but the setting of *Song of a Red Morning* has some basis in reality.

Dunpeldyr was a large late iron age hill-fort. Possibly meaning Fort of the Stockades or Spear-shafts, it was situated on a prominent hill in East Lothian now known as Traprain Law. It was occupied during the late Iron Age from about 40 AD to 400 AD, an occupation that spanned the period of Roman occupation of Britain and ended when the Angles began to expand northwards from their territory in the south. Dunpeldyr was probably the stronghold of a tribe known to the Romans as the Votadini, a tribe which went on to form the basis of the kingdom of the Gododdin, which also had strongholds at Dun Eidyn (Edinburgh) and Dun Gefryn (Yeavering Bell).

Traprain Law is famous for the find, in the early part of the 20th century, of a hoard of Roman silver dating from the later period of Roman occupation. There are many beautiful things in the hoard (some are on display at the National Museum of Scotland in Edinburgh) but much of the treasure is in the form of hack-silver – crushed and hacked to pieces. Why it had been buried and where it came from, whether stolen in a raid or a payment for services rendered, is a matter for speculation. *Song of a Red Morning* is a fictional exploration of one possible explanation.

Dunpeldyr Law is also the setting for the first of a series of as yet unpublished novels which make up *The Trystan Trilogy*. The first volume of the Trilogy, *The Wolf in Winter*, published in 2021, takes place at the end of the 5th century and explores the relationship between characters taken from the Arthurian legend of Tristan and Isolde, here reclaimed for Scotland. Read the first part of the book in the pages that follow.

BONUS MATERIAL

Extract from *The Trystan Trilogy*, Volume I

THE WOLF IN WINTER

Dunpeldyr in Lothian

Spring 491 AD

Tomorrow, I will burn my father.

Tomorrow, I'll set flame to his pyre and send the smoke of his burning high into the sky. Men will see that smoke from Dun Eidyn in the west to the eastern lands the Angles have taken for their own, and know he's dead, the man who ruled Lothian for over thirty years. But Lothian won't remain unruled for long. Tomorrow, once the fire has burned away to ash, the Chieftains will gather in Dunpeldyr's hall to choose another king. They'll argue and bicker, remember old feuds and settle new scores, debate the rights of this one or that, declaim their qualities and ancestry. Yet I will say nothing and none will speak my name. I'll sit in the chair that stands beside my father's, the one I've made my own, and let his ashes sift through my fingers until they've talked themselves into a decision. For they have little choice and I will have none.

So, tomorrow, I will be King, but tonight I'm free. Tonight, I'll pace Dunpeldyr's ramparts and watch the sun bleed behind the sloe-black peaks of Manau until all light and warmth have vanished from the world. Tonight, in the cold and dark, I'll tell myself the story of everything that has led me here, before that too vanishes. Already my tale is that of a man I no longer know, a man whose name, amongst others, was Corwynal of Lothian. Tomorrow, that man will step over the threshold the fickle gods have forced him to cross. But tonight he'll remember the night of Imbolc more than a score of years before when he made a choice of his own and stepped over another threshold. So that's where he'll begin – on a Night of Thresholds when he still had a father, but not yet a brother.

Or a son.

····· CHAPTER ONE ·····

Dunpeldyr in Lothian

Spring 468 AD

Corwynal flinched as yet another scream knifed through Dunpeldyr's empty hall. The cry shrieked up into the smoke-stained rafters, before dwindling to a low moaning echo that trickled away to dusty silence. Eventually, however, other sounds slipped back into the hall; snow creaked on the thatch, women murmured anxiously in the chamber at the end of the hall, and, in the distance, borne on the wintry east wind, the sounds of celebration rose from the lambing fields.

Corwynal should have been down in those fields with the rest of the men of Dunpeldyr, for it was the night of Imbolc, the night that marked the end of winter. Instead, he was listening to a woman scream in a cold hall lit only by a handful of little lamps, though, in truth, he had no choice. He was Captain of the woman's guard, and his duty was to protect her, although, right then, he couldn't guard her from what was happening beyond the leather hangings at the end of the hall because no-one could. And now it had begun to seem as if he was no longer there to witness the birth he'd expected, but the death he feared. Night edged its way toward dawn, and each scream was weaker than the last, each silence longer, until it was the silence rather than the screams that burned through his blood and bones.

If he'd been alone, he would have raised his fists to shake them at the gods and demand they do something for once. He might even have begged. But he wasn't alone. His men waited with him, men with more right than him to guard the woman, for they, like her, were from Galloway. They were hard, these men, their faces scarred and evil, their weapons honed to a gleam. They lived and breathed battle, laughed at its bowel-churning terror, yet still they flinched at a woman's screams.

Corwynal, as their leader, had to be harder than any of them. He had to hold his stance, head back, feet apart, one hand clenched so tightly on the pommel of his sword his nails had driven into his flesh, leaving his palm sticky with blood. He had to pretend this meant nothing to him, and so he gripped his expression just as fiercely. Perhaps he fooled his men, for none of them spoke, though he felt their breath pluming on the back of his neck as they muttered curses or prayers. He heard them move restlessly behind him as if they too wished they were far away, down by the Imbolc fires, drinking and feasting to drive away the dark.

In Lothian, as in all the Lands between the Walls, Imbolc, the Night of Thresholds, was a night for men to sing and shout and stagger back to the arms of their women in the bitter dawn of the first day of spring. But the Galloway men didn't complain. Instead, they waited, bracing themselves for each scream to rise out of the anxious murmur of the woman's attendants, until Tegid, the youngest, unable to bear it any longer, whimpered in distress, and Corwynal came at last to a decision.

'This can't go on.' He turned to face his men for the first time that night and jerked his head at Tegid. 'Fetch Blaize.'

The Galloway men exchanged glances, and in the dim light of the flickering Imbolc lamps Corwynal saw Tegid pale.

'But where? And what—?'

'Just find him!' Corwynal's voice began to crack open, but he caught and held it.

Tell him She's dying. 'She.' That was how he thought of her. She needed no other name, though of course she had one. His men would have called her Princess Gwenllian, the Fair Flower of Galloway, for she was sister to Marc, Galloway's King. But she was Queen of Lothian now and soon to give birth to its heir, for she was wed to the King – who was Corwynal's father.

Time passed, then more time, as he waited for Blaize to come and wondered if he'd done the right thing in sending for his uncle. A birth was a women's battle to fight, and Blaize had little patience with women. But, after a day and night of screaming, Blaize, with healing skills, might be her only hope.

The embers in the firepit dwindled to a smoor of ruddy ash that gave little light and no warmth at all. Some of the Imbolc lamps guttered and died and sent greasy smoke spiralling into the rafters. The stench of mutton-fat merged with the stink of stale rushes and the harsher, acrid smell of whatever was happening at the other end of the hall. Somewhere, a shutter banged as the wind rose, and within the hall the wall-hangings stirred in the draughts, setting the woven wolves, Lothian's symbol, slinking through the shadows as if they were alive, their jewelled eyes glinting balefully. The remaining Imbolc lamps flickered and waned but, like Corwynal's hopes, couldn't quite be extinguished. As long as he waited, witnessing her pain, she wouldn't die, *couldn't* die. Not when she was only eighteen, a bride of a mere eight months.

It was close to dawn when Tegid returned, slipping back to take his place with the others and throwing Corwynal a guilty, apprehensive glance as he did so. Behind him the door crashed open, and snow plumed into the hall on a blast of icy Imbolc air that smelled of pine and heather. The wind drove back the stench of smoke and rushes, and most of the lamps blew out, turning the man who stood in the doorway into a hard-edged silhouette set against the streaming torchlight of the courtyard. Corwynal's heart began to thud, for he knew that silhouette all too well. It wasn't Blaize who'd come, but another man entirely.

Rifallyn, King of Lothian, his father and Blaize's half-brother, ordered his men to wait outside, then slammed the door behind him and strode over to the firepit, stripping off his gloves as he did so to thrust his hands out to the faintly glowing ash. The Galloway men straightened and stared into the middle distance, hoping to make themselves invisible. Perhaps they succeeded, for the King ignored them and gazed down into the fire, a tall man, broad across the shoulders, his bulk accentuated by a shrouding cloak of wolf-skin.

'Well?' he asked, lifting his head. His tone was mild, but his expression mirrored that of the snarling wolf's head on his gold-embroidered tunic. More gold glinted from his wrists and neck, from the grip of his sword and the jewelled brooch on his shoulder. Yet none of these could compete with the glitter of his amber wolf's eyes. 'Well, Corwynal?' he repeated, his voice not quite steady, and Corwynal began to be afraid, and not just for himself.

'The Queen is come early to the birth,' he replied as evenly as he could, with a deliberate glance at his men to remind his father of what was at stake. 'But her women say it goes badly.'

The sound of the women was louder now, and one of them was sobbing noisily. His father turned and spat into the fire. 'Women!' He threw his gloves to the floor and, thrusting aside one of the Galloway men, strode over to Corwynal and loomed over him. 'What do they know? What do *you* know? Tell me that!' He took Corwynal's upper arm in a painful grip, his fingers digging into the flesh above his bronze armband. 'What has any of this to do with *me?*'

'Rather a lot, I would have thought,' said a voice from behind them.

The Galloway men, who hadn't noticed Blaize come into the hall, hissed and backed away, though, to Corwynal's eyes, the man who strolled towards them looked harmless enough. He was of medium height and of middle years, with a northern look to him, for, like Corwynal, he was half-Caledonian. His long greying dark hair was pulled back into a silver ring and he was dressed in a none-too-clean habit such as those worn by the priests of Chrystos, though he didn't follow that god. Blaize served older gods; around his neck hung an oak-leaf medallion, and his forehead bore the faded mark of the druids. Corwynal's men believed him to be a Caledonian sorcerer, but he thought of his uncle as a friend, one of the few he had.

'You married the girl,' Blaize reminded his half-brother. 'You wanted her to give you a son, and so . . .' He shrugged. 'So, here we are . . .'

'Indeed!' Rifallyn snarled, but he slackened his grip on Corwynal's arm. 'Well then, since you've chosen to interfere, you can see that she does.'

Blaize held the King's eyes for a moment, then smiled his wintry smile, loosened the knife in the sheath at his waist, walked to the end of the hall and pushed aside the hangings that barred the entrance to the women's chambers. Moments later, three of the Queen's attendants came stumbling out to throw themselves at Rifallyn's feet, sobbing and begging for his protection from the druid priest, and reaching up to touch his tunic in entreaty, their hands slick with blood and mucus.

'Get out!' the King snapped, stepping back sharply, his voice thick with disgust, and the women scuttled off into the night, keening as they went. *Is She dead?* There was no longer any sound from the bedchamber where a woman had been screaming; all Corwynal could hear was the ragged breathing of his men and his own heart thudding in his chest. Then a fresh cry came from beyond the hangings, and his heart stopped entirely. It wasn't the scream he'd braced himself for, nor the lasting silence he dreaded more.

It was the faint, querulous wail of an infant.

About the Author

I was born, and still live, in Scotland on the shores of a river, between the mountains and the sea. I'm a retired scientist and science administrator but have always been fascinated by the early history of Scotland, and I love fleshing out that history with the stories of fictional, and not-so-fictional, characters.

Song of a Red Morning was first published as an e-book by Amazon in 2019. In 2020 a collection of my short stories, *The Man who Loved Landscape and other stories*, was published by Amazon, and was followed, in 2021, by a collection of poetry, *The Ghost in the Machine*.

Song of a Red Morning is set at Dunpeldyr, the Iron Age Fort of Traprain Law in East Lothian. This is also the setting for the opening of my Dark-age Trilogy, *The Trystan Trilogy*, which consists of *The Wolf in Winter, The Swan in Summer* and *The Serpent in Spring*. *The Wolf in Winter* is my first full-length novel and was published in 2021.

Find out more about me and my writing on my website:

Barbaralennox.com

Connect with me on the following:

Twitter	twitter.com/barbaralennox4
Instagram	instagram.com/barbaralennoxwriter
Pinterest	pinterest.co.uk/barbaralennox58
Goodreads	goodreads.com/author/show/19661962.Barbara_Lennox
Amazon	viewauthor.at/authorprofile

I very much hope you've enjoyed reading these stories. If you have, I'd love to hear from you, so **please post a review on Amazon**. It needn't be an essay – a couple of lines would be fantastic. Reviews are particularly helpful for new authors like me.

SUBSCRIBE TO MY NEWSLETTER

at

Barbaralennox.com/subscribe

for a **FREE SHORT STORY**, exclusive novel extracts, notifications of new blog posts and new content on my website, together with regular Newsletters about my writing journey.

Visit my website **www.barbaralennox.com** for more free stories, extracts from my forthcoming novels, sample poems, and lots of information about my Dark-age Trilogy.

ALSO BY BARBARA LENNOX

*T*he Wolf in Winter is the first part of a thrilling retelling of the Tristan and Isolde legend, set amidst the warring cultures of dark age Scotland. The following books in *The Trystan Trilogy, The Swan in Summer* and *The Serpent in Spring* will be published in 2022 and 2023 respectively.

To find out more about this collection visit: getbook.at/Wolfinwinter or scan the code

*T*he Man who Loved Landscape: A collection of short stories which explore the many facets of loss, from the loss of a loved one or love itself, to the loss of faith, self-respect, identity, innocence, or even life. The stories are broad in scope, setting and tone, but in all of them the characters confront loss with wry humour and a determination to explore what it means to be alive. Published in 2020.

A simply astonishing book of forty short stories. Beautifully written, the tales flow one to the other, sometimes with no discernible connection other than a common theme of the natural environment of the British Isles – with a strong bias to the Scottish Highlands. Julia Blake, Author of *Black Ice*.

To find out more about this collection visit: getbook.at/Manwholovedlandscape or scan the code.

*T*he Ghost in the Machine: A collection of poems that explore the natural world, the past, scientific ideas and the human condition. Topics range from a fossil bird to a mythical tree, and from the inheritance pattern of comb shape in chickens to the final journey we all have to make. Published in 2021.

Barbara Lennox observes the natural world with loving and critical detail and analyses what she observes through the lens of a poet and philosopher. She speaks of the profound and shows us illuminating flashes of the ghost in the machine, the spirit of all living things, the delicate balance of life and death, endurance and extinction, pure joy and bittersweet loss. We not only experience the ghost; we are of the ghost ourselves. Sherry L Ross, Author of *Seeds of the Pomegranate.*

To find out more about this collection visit: getbook.at/theghostinthemachine or scan the code.

ACKNOWLEDGEMENTS

I would never have written *Song of a Red Morning* or *The Trystan Trilogy* if I hadn't attended the 'Continuing as a Writer' classes, part of the University of Dundee's Continuing Education Programme. These classes were tutored by Esther Read whose support and encouragement has been unstinting and invaluable. Esther, I can't thank you enough. I'm also grateful to the other members of the class, and the Nethergate Writers Group, for their helpful and constructive criticism.

At home, Harry, Rambo and Oscar, the best cats in the world, were with me all the way, usually asleep.

Finally, but not least, I'd like to thank my husband, Will, for putting up with all the scribbling and not asking any questions.

Printed in Great Britain
by Amazon